WARNING!
SCAREDY SQUIRREL INSISTS
THAT THIS BOOK NOT BE READ
IN BATHROOMS.

READER SECURITY QUIZ

1. I HOLD BOOKS WITH...

- HANDS ☐ (1 point)
- SHARP CLAWS ☐ (0 points)
- SLIMY TENTACLES ☐ (0 points)

2. SQUIRRELS ARE...

- OVERRATED ☐ (0 points)
- FUN TO CHASE ☐ (-1 point)
- LOVABLE RODENTS ☐ (1 point)

3. I SMELL GOOD...

- SORT OF ☐ (0 points)
- ONLY ON SPECIAL OCCASIONS ☐ (0 points)
- ALL YEAR LONG ☐ (1 point)

4. S.O.S. STANDS FOR...

- SMALL ONION SOUP ☐ (0 points)
- SAVE OUR SOULS ☐ (1 point)
- SCAREDY ORVILLE SQUIRREL ☐ (1 point)

CONGRATULATIONS!
IF YOUR TOTAL POINTS ARE BETWEEN 1 AND 6, YOU CAN SAFELY PROCEED TO THE NEXT PAGE.

Scaredy Squirrel

In a Nutshell

A Stepping Stone Book™

Random House New York

 Published in the United States by Random House Children's Books, a division of Penguin Random House LLC, New York. Originally published in hardcover in the United States by Random House Children's Books, a division of Penguin Random House LLC, New York, in 2021. Published simultaneously in Canada by Tundra Books, Toronto, in 2021.

Random House and the colophon are registered trademarks and A Stepping Stone Book and the colophon are trademarks of Penguin Random House LLC.

Visit us on the Web! rhcbooks.com

Educators and librarians, for a variety of teaching tools,
visit us at RHTeachersLibrarians.com

The Library of Congress has cataloged the hardcover edition of this work as follows:
Names: Watt, Melanie, author, illustrator. | Title: Scaredy Squirrel in a nutshell / by Melanie Watt. | Description: First edition. | New York : Random House Children's Books, 2021. | Series: [Scaredy Squirrel ; 1] | Audience: Ages 6–9. | Summary: Scaredy has spent his life defending his tree from UFOs, lumberjacks, mammoths, and more, so when (possibly poison) Ivy the rabbit sends a note he must calculate the risks of friendship. | Identifiers: LCCN 2020032029 (print) | LCCN 2020032030 (ebook) | ISBN 978-0-593-30755-7 (hardcover) | ISBN 978-0-593-30756-4 (lib. bdg.) |
ISBN 978-0-593-30757-1 (ebook)
Subjects: CYAC: Fear—Fiction. | Squirrels—Fiction. | Rabbits—Fiction. | Friendship—Fiction. | Classification: LCC PZ7.W3323 Sc 2021 (print) | LCC PZ7.W3323 (ebook) | DDC [E]—dc23

ISBN 978-0-593-56845-3 (paperback)

MANUFACTURED IN CHINA
10 9 8 7 6 5 4 3 2 1
First Paperback Edition 2022

NUTTY CONTENTS

CHAPTER 1
SAFE AND SOUND

SCAREDY SQUIRREL
WATCHES OVER HIS
NUT TREE.

A FEW TRESPASSERS SCAREDY SQUIRREL IS AFRAID COULD DROP BY:

MAMMOTHS

WOODPECKERS

MUST BEAM UP TREE!
ALIENS
MUST BUILD CABIN WITH TREE!
LUMBERJACKS
MUST SHARPEN CLAWS ON TREE!
CATS
MUST TERMINATE TREE!
TERMITES

SO HE'S BEEN GOING OUT ON A LIMB TO SECURE THE AREA.

THIS PAGE IS BLANK FOR SUPERSTITIOUS REASONS.

SCAREDY SQUIRREL BEGAN PROTECTING
HIS NUT TREE AT AN EARLY AGE.
WARNING!
CUTE FACTOR MIGHT BE
OVERWHELMING FOR SOME.
WOODEN
TRAIN
SIDETRACKS
TERMITES

TRAFFIC CONE
FENDS OFF
ALIENS

AS SCAREDY'S NUT TREE GREW, SO DID HIS SAFETY MEASURES.

DISCO BALL
GARDEN GNOME
PROS:
OBJECTS DISTRACT TRESPASSERS
CONS:
OBJECTS ATTRACT DUST, AND DUST GATHERS . . .

DUST BUNNIES
(ACCORDING TO SCAREDY SQUIRREL)
MUST SPREAD DUST AROUND TREE!
SIGNALS A BUNCH OF DUSTY SIBLINGS WITH ANTENNAE
DIGS BURROWS
SNEEZES
ADORABLE POM-POM TAIL
97% SURE THEY'RE PALS WITH GARY

LUCKILY, SCAREDY KNOWS HOW TO KEEP THINGS CLEAN WITH A . . .

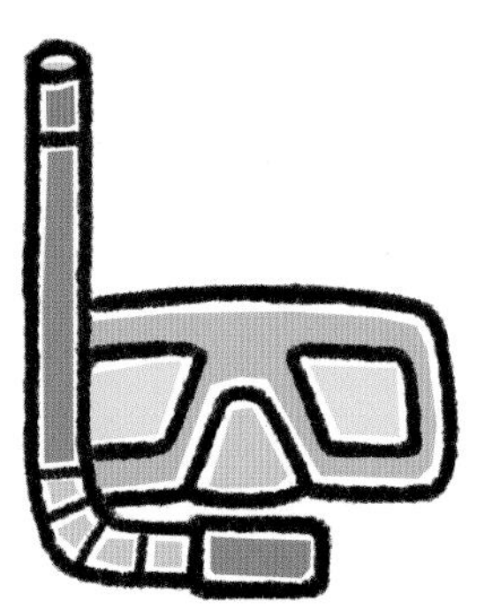

SCUBA MASK

DUST-REPELLENT SUIT

PAIR OF RUBBER GLOVES

VACUUM

SCAREDY SQUIRREL
VACUUMS . . .

AND VACUUMS . . .
AND VACUUMS . . .
WHEN SUDDENLY . . .
THE VACUUM CLOGS!

A FEW ITEMS THAT COULD BE AT THE BOTTOM OF THIS:

A. WOOL

B. FEATHERS

C. BOLTS AND SCREWS

D. MUSTACHES

E. HAIRBALLS

F. WOOD CHIPS

HE MUST UNCLOG
THIS VACUUM BEFORE
THE DUST SETTLES IN!

TOP SECRET

SCAREDY'S SWIFT UNCLOGGING PLAN

STEP 1: PANIC

STEP 2: SLIDE DOWN VACUUM

STEP 3: LIFT VACUUM NOZZLE

STEP 4: UNCLOG IT WITH PLUNGER

STEP 5: HURRY BACK UP TREE

STEP 6: RESUME VACUUMING

DO NOT STEP ON GROUND

MAYDAY!
Shedding woolly mammoths like to scratch their behinds on icy, snow-covered trees!

MOVE FAST!
Lumberjacks may be twirling their mustaches near tempting sign.

PLAID SALE!!!
(IN THE CITY)

LOOK OUT!
Aliens want to beam up everything! If spaceship hovers too long, loose bolts, nuts and screws can drop to the ground!
I AM HERE.
ALERT!
Woodpeckers cannot stand the glare of mirrors. If they come a-knocking, feathers will fly!
CAREFUL!
Wooden train is packed with wood chips and dizzy termites.
REMEMBER!
This sturdy security guard is on duty!
DANGER!
Stepping on a hairball can lead to a mushy mess!
CLOG IS IN HERE.
ACHOO!
NOTE TO SELF: IF ALL ELSE FAILS, PLAY DEAD FOR 2 HOURS, THEN DUST YOURSELF OFF!

AS PLANNED,
SCAREDY SLIDES
DOWN THE VACUUM.

THEN HE CAREFULLY LIFTS UP THE NOZZLE...
AND DISCOVERS SOMETHING MORE TERRIFYING THAN HE HAD EVER IMAGINED...

AN ADORABLE POM-POM TAIL!!!
CATCHING A DUST BUNNY WAS NOT PART OF THE PLAN!

SCAREDY RACES BACK UP THE TREE AND KNOCKS DOWN THE VACUUM...
WHICH KNOCKS OFF THE DISCO BALL...
WHICH KNOCKS THE GNOME...
WHICH KNOCKS INTO THE TREE...

AND KNOCKS OUT EVERY SINGLE NUT!

SCAREDY SQUIRREL PANICS AND . . .

PLAYS DEAD.

ARE YOU OKAY?
?

HEY...
IS THAT A
DUST-FREE
BUNNY?
HEY...
IS THAT?

YIPPEE!!!
FOUND MY
EARMUFFS!

2 HOURS LATER...

SCAREDY SQUIRREL
WANTS TO EAT A NUT.

BUT TO GET A NUT,
HE MUST SET FOOT ON
DANGEROUS GROUND.

A FEW POSSIBLE RUN-INS THAT MAKE THIS A RISKY MOVE:

THE BUNNY
(ACCORDING TO SCAREDY SQUIRREL)
MUST MAKE EYE CONTACT WITH SQUIRREL!
WEARS EARMUFFS THAT CLOG VACUUMS
ASKS IF ALL IS OKAY
STILL ATTACHED TO AN ADORABLE POM-POM TAIL
63% SURE IT KNOWS GARY

SO STEPPING OUT IS NOT AN OPTION!

Scaredy's TO-DO List:
Wait an entire year for new nuts to grow in.
Fall
Summer
Winter
Spring
In the meantime, order takeout!

A FEW SNACKS ON SCAREDY'S DINING PLAN:

NUT OVER EASY

NUT TACO

NUT KEBAB

NUT SANDWICH

FORTUNATELY,
THIS SQUIRREL ALWAYS
HAS A PLAN B . . .

PLAN B:
PIZZA
HELLO, MAY I PLACE AN ORDER?
ONE SMALL PIZZA WITH CASHEWS, PLEASE.
DROP OFF BELOW THE NUT TREE.

31 MINUTES LATER...
HMMM.
NUT TREE?
WHERE?
PIZZA
SCAREDY'S DELIVERY
GETS DROPPED OFF...
IN THE
WRONG
SPOT!
PIZZA
PILE OF NUTS,
CLOSE
ENOUGH!
PLAID SALE,
HERE
I COME!
PIZZA
ANY WAY YOU SLICE IT,
SCAREDY WILL HAVE TO
SET FOOT ON THE GROUND.
THIS IS RISKY ON A WHOLE
OTHER LEVEL!

SCAREDY'S
GROUND-LEVEL GET-UP:
SAFETY HELMET
T. REX GRABBER TOOL
ELBOW PADS
KNEE PADS
STILTS
DO NOT STEP ON GROUND
1. MARCH TOWARD THE PIZZA BOX
2. OPEN BOX WITH GRABBER TOOL
3. GRAB A SLICE WITH GRABBER TOOL
4. HURRY BACK UP TREE, EAT SLICE
5. REPEAT STEPS UNTIL BOX IS EMPTY
NOTE TO SELF: IF IT ALL FALLS FLAT, PLAY DEAD!

SCAREDY STARTS MARCHING...
HE APPROACHES THE PIZZA...
PIZZA
PIZZA
AND LEANS IN TO OPEN THE BOX WHEN...

PIZZA
HI! WHAT'S UP?
AHHH!

SCAREDY SCRAMBLES TO SAFETY AND PLAYS DEAD.

2 HOURS LATER...

SCAREDY SQUIRREL
IS HUNGRY FOR
ANSWERS.
PIZZA

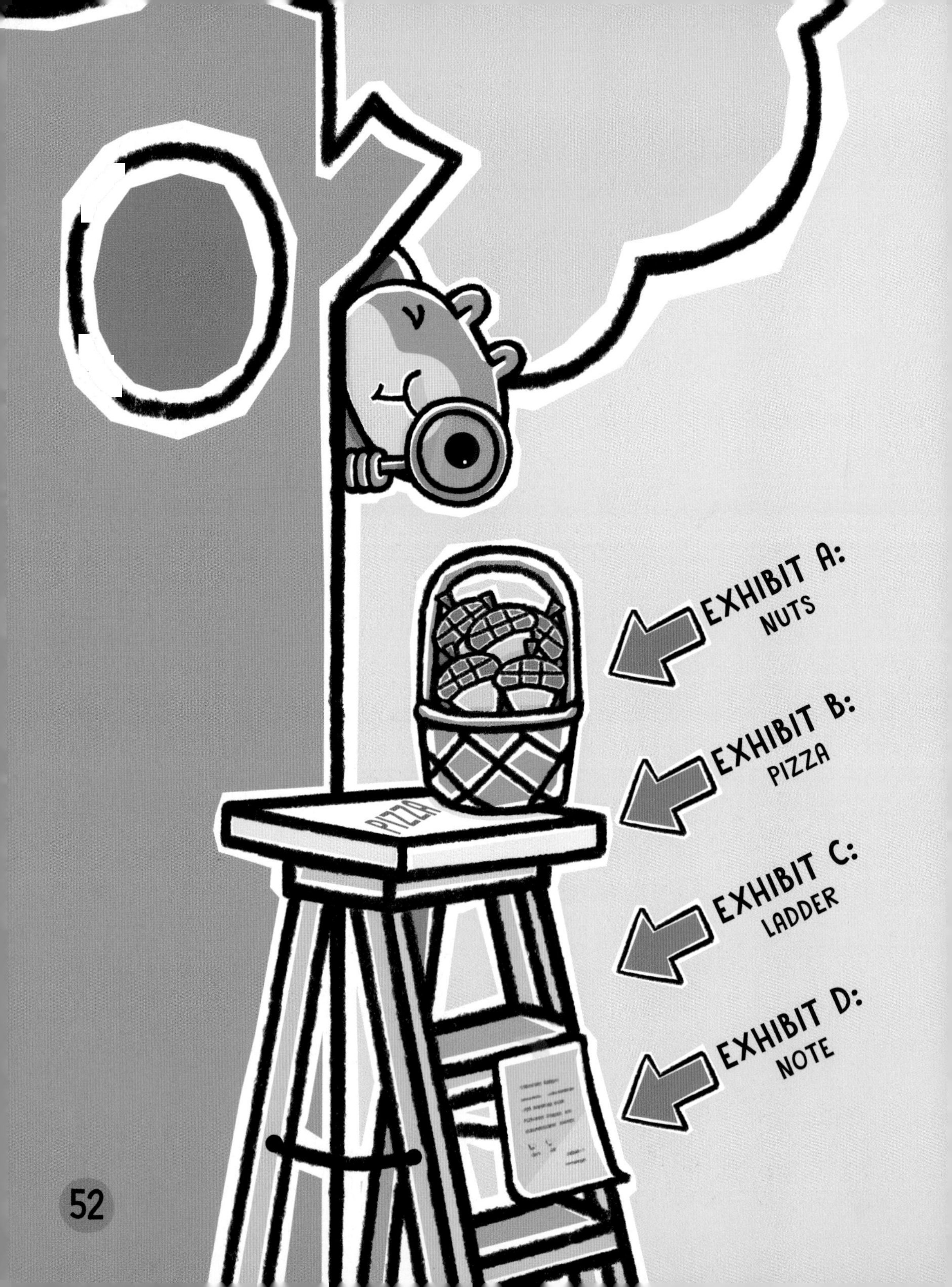
EXHIBIT A:
NUTS
EXHIBIT B:
PIZZA
EXHIBIT C:
LADDER
EXHIBIT D:
NOTE
PIZZA

TO AVOID PAPER CUTS, SCAREDY PUTS ON HIS OVEN MITTS.

SCAREDY SQUIRREL IS STUMPED. HE MUST CALCULATE THE RISKS BEFORE HE CAN ANSWER IVY.

RISKS:

1. Ivy might be **poisonous!** (name makes me itchy)

2. Ivy might really be **Gary** in disguise!

3. Ivy might be a **spy** searching for my classified information!

4. Ivy and I might have **nothing** in common!!!

BENEFITS:
1. Ivy is NOT a dust bunny.
2. Ivy is kind to my tree.
I
3. Ivy is friendly to me.
LET'S CHAT!
4. Ivy unclogs vacuums.
5. Ivy is helpful.
PIZZA
6. Ivy smiles.
7. Ivy is peaceful.
8. Ivy has impeccable handwriting!
(a rare skill nowadays)

AFTER CAREFUL THOUGHT, SCAREDY CONCLUDES THAT THE REALISTIC BENEFITS OUTWEIGH THE UNLIKELY RISKS.
IN A NUTSHELL:
IVY = SAFE
SCAREDY HANDS OVER HIS ANSWER.
OKAY . . .
A BIT STRANGE.
BUT WORKS FOR ME!
Yes
Let's meet halfway and split a pizza at half past 5!

A FEW LAST-MINUTE DETAILS SCAREDY MUST HANDLE BEFORE 5:30 P.M.:

MEASURING TAPE

NAME TAGS

TOOTHPASTE

RADIO

HAND SANITIZER

NAPKINS

4:52 P.M. SCAREDY MEASURES THE HALFWAY SPOT.
5:07 P.M. HE PREPARES AN ID VERIFICATION TEST.
HELLO
MY NAME IS
HELLO
MY NAME IS
HELLO
MY NAME IS
Ivy
5:09 P.M. HE BRUSHES HIS TEETH.
MINT
5:12 P.M. HE PLAYS ELEVATOR MUSIC AND WAITS.
SERIOUSLY?

SCAREDY EAGERLY OPENS THE BOX . . .

ANCHOVIES!
AHHH!!
AHH!!
HELLO

2 MINUTES LATER, THEY REALIZE...

OKAY, SO THEY DON'T HAVE THAT MUCH IN COMMON.
BUT SCAREDY IS STILL GLAD HE MET A NEW FRIEND!

SCAREDY AND IVY HAVE A PICNIC...

THEY CHAT...

AND THEY WATCH THE SUNSET.

...PIZZA!!!
WE FORGOT THE PIZZA! IVY! LET'S HURRY UP AND CATAPULT IT OUT INTO SPACE BEFORE IT ATTRACTS A HERD OF HUNGRY ANCHOVY-LOVING FLAMINGOS!!
HELLO MY NAME IS Scaredy
HELLO
OR . . . WE COULD JUST CALL MY FRIEND TIM!
[crickets chirping]
HELLO
TIM LOVES ANCHOVIES! HE ADORES TREES! DON'T WORRY, SCAREDY. YOU'LL BOTH GET ALONG SO WELL!!!
TIM IS SHORT FOR TIMOTHY, RIGHT?
HELLO MY NAME IS Scaredy
HELLO MY NAME IS Timothy
UH . . . NOT EXACTLY?

TIMBER!!!
COME OVER AND MEET SCAREDY . . . AND GRAB A BITE!
OKEY-DOKEY!
Scaredy
PIZZA

TIMBER
(ACCORDING TO SCAREDY SQUIRREL)
MUST BUILD A DAM WITH TREE!
HAS AN APPETITE FOR BARK AND COLD ANCHOVY PIZZA
FLAT-OUT TERRIFYING
99% SURE HE HAS GARY'S PHONE NUMBER

HELLO MY NAME IS Scaredy
IS SCAREDY OKAY?
WAS IT SOMETHING I SAID?
OH... WE'LL FIND OUT IN EXACTLY 2 HOURS!
HELLO MY NAME IS Ivy
THE END

FAQ
(FREQUENTLY ASKED QUESTIONS)
Q1 SCAREDY, WILL YOU BE BACK WITH NEW NUTTY ADVENTURES?
S.O.S.: YES!!! I have plenty to be afraid of ... like Vikings, clams, yetis, bookworms and Gary.
MUST POKE SQUIRREL!
Q2 SCAREDY, WHO'S THIS GARY YOU KEEP MENTIONING?
S.O.S.: A clingy germ rival who dates from waaay back.
GA-GA GRRR!
Q3 WHERE CAN I FIND A SCAREDY SQUIRREL BOBBLEHEAD?
S.O.S.: Hopefully, nowhere!!!
Just the thought makes me dizzy!
SORRY TO INTERRUPT, BUT IS THERE ANY PIZZA LEFT?
Q4 SCAREDY, WHY AREN'T YOU LIKE A TYPICAL TREE SQUIRREL?
S.O.S.: Because I'm not a typical tree squirrel — I'm atypical!
And that's what makes my adventures so incredibly fun!
Q5 SCAREDY, CAN YOU LIST ALL OF YOUR PICTURE BOOKS?
S.O.S.:
• Scaredy Squirrel
• Scaredy Squirrel Makes a Friend
• Scaredy Squirrel at the Beach
• Scaredy Squirrel at Night
• Scaredy Squirrel Has a Birthday Party
• Scaredy Squirrel Goes Camping
... and more to come!
WATCH OUT FOR PAPER CUTS!